Unicorn Day

Words by **Diana Murray**
Pictures by **Luke Flowers**

sourcebooks
jabberwocky

For Kate and Jane, who played among unicorns.
—DM

For Josh McGeehan, a one-of-a-kind friend, who always
encouraged me to be myself, and accepted me just as I was.
You brought rocket fuel to those wacky early years of this
creative journey. Forever grateful. Forever BIRDHEADS.
—LF

Text © 2019 by Diana Murray · Illustrations © 2019 by Luke Flowers · Cover and internal design © 2019 by Sourcebooks, Inc.
Sourcebooks and the colophon are registered trademarks of Sourcebooks, Inc. All rights reserved. · The characters and events
portrayed in this book are fictitious or are used fictitiously. Any similarity to real persons, living or dead, is purely coincidental
and not intended by the author. · The full color art was sketched and painted in Photoshop using a wide range of unique digital
brushes. · Published by Sourcebooks Jabberwocky, an imprint of Sourcebooks, Inc. · P.O. Box 4410, Naperville, Illinois 60567-
4410 · (630) 961-3900 · Fax: (630) 961-2168 · sourcebooks.com · Library of Congress Cataloging-in-Publication Data is on file
with the publisher. · Source of Production: Shenzhen Wing King Tong Paper Products Co. Ltd., Shenzhen, Guangdong Province,
China · Date of Production: March 2019 · Run Number: 5014193 · Printed and bound in China.
WKT 10 9 8 7 6 5 4 3 2 1

When unicorns come out to play they have three rules they must obey:

UNICORN DAY RULES

RULE NUMBER ONE:
Show off your horn.
Be proud to be a unicorn!

RULE NUMBER TWO:
Fluff up that hair!
Make sure it's groomed
and styled with flair.

RULE NUMBER THREE:
Have fun, fun, fun!
(This rule's the most important one.)

In the woods,
where tall trees sway,
they sing the song
of Unicorn Day.

Sunshine, flowers, fairy wings,
today's a day for joyful things!

Neigh, neigh, neigh! Dance and play!
Happy, happy unicorn Day!

They kick their hooves,
they jump and cheer…

and sparkly butterflies flutter near!

They slide on rainbows in the air...

and love to braid
each other's hair.

They point their horns up
as they fly
and cupcakes rain down
from the sky!

Then after they
have had a bite,
it's time to have…

a Glitter

That's a horse!

He turns around
to leave, of course.

His horn's not real.
It's just pretend.

But they don't want
to lose a friend!

They tie the horn back on his head and give the horse a hug instead.

Then it's back to...

fun, fun, fun!
(That rule's the most
important one.)

They march together,
tall and proud,
and soon...

some *more* friends join the crowd!

Clip-clip-clop!
They trot along
as everybody
sings the song.

Cupcakes, sprinkles, cherry tarts,
starlight twinkles, glowing hearts,

Sunshine, flowers, fairy wings, today's a day for joyful things! Neigh, neigh, neigh! Dance and play!